This book belongs to

....

Illustrated by: Erica-Jane Waters
Reading consultant: Geraldine Taylor

Marks and Spencer plc
PO Box 3339
Chester CH99 9QS

shop online
www.marksandspencer.com

ISBN 978-1-78061-708-4
Printed in China

M&S
First Readers

Hansel
and
Gretel

M&S

Five steps for enjoyable reading

Traditional stories and fairy tales are a great way to begin reading practice. The stories and characters are familiar and lively. Follow the steps below to help your child become a confident and independent reader:

Step 1
Read the story aloud to your child. Run your finger under the words as you read.

This story begins with someone's tummy rumbling! Little Hansel and Gretel hadn't had any food to eat. They were very hungry.

Hansel and Gretel heard their mean old aunty whisper to their father.

"Get rid of the children," she said. "Then we will have enough to eat."

8

Step 2
Look at the pictures and talk about what is happening.

Step 3

Read the simple text on the right-hand page together. When reading, some words come up again and again, such as **the**, **to**, **and**. Your child will quickly get to recognize these high-frequency words by sight.

The children were
nd and hungry. They
idn't know what to do.

Step 4

When your child is ready, encourage them to read the simple lines on their own.

Step 5

Help your child to complete the puzzles at the back of the book.

This story begins with someone's tummy rumbling! Little Hansel and Gretel hadn't had any food to eat. They were very hungry.

Hansel and Gretel heard their mean old aunty whisper to their father.

"Get rid of the children," she said. "Then we will have enough to eat."

The children were
sad and hungry. They
didn't know what to do.

The next day, the children were led into the woods. Soon they were far from home. But Hansel was clever! He had a crust of bread and left a trail of crumbs.

"I have a plan," Hansel told Gretel.

Hansel and Gretel were left
all alone in the dark woods.
"Don't worry," said Hansel.
"We will follow the trail of bread
home again!" But a little bird
had eaten all the bread.
Now they were lost!

"Don't worry, Gretel," said Hansel, bravely. "I will look after you."

Before long it got dark.
Hansel and Gretel made
a little fire to keep warm.
There were strange noises
in the woods. They were
too hungry and scared
to go to sleep.

T-wit-t-woo!

"What was that?" cried Gretel.

"It was an owl," said Hansel.

The next day, Hansel and Gretel wandered through the woods, until they came to a funny little house. "It's made of sweets," said Gretel.

They stopped to eat a bit of the little house.

17

Suddenly, an old woman came out.

"Who is eating my little house?" asked the old woman.

"Sorry," said Hansel. "We didn't know it was your house."

"We were very hungry," said Gretel.

"I will give you ham and jam,"
said the old woman.

So Hansel and Gretel went inside the little house. The old woman gave Hansel and Gretel a big supper and sent them off to bed.

But Gretel did not go to sleep. She heard the old woman cackling to herself. She was really a witch! And she had a wicked plan. "I will feed the boy to make him big and fat. Then I will eat him up!"

Gretel told Hansel about the
witch's plan.

The next day, the old witch locked Hansel in a cage. The witch made Gretel give Hansel lots of food to make him fat. But Gretel was clever. She had a plan. The old witch could not see very well. Gretel gave Hansel an old bone, to pretend it was his finger.

"Hmm, not fat yet!"
thought the witch.

23

One day, the old witch couldn't wait any longer.

"Fat or not, Hansel will be my dinner," she cackled.

"But the oven isn't hot," said Gretel.

"Nonsense," said the witch and she opened the oven. Quick as a flash, Gretel pushed her in and closed the door.

And that was the
end of the witch!

At last, Hansel and Gretel escaped from the witch's house. And can you guess who was looking for them? The children's father found them in the woods and took them home. The mean old aunty had gone away and they never saw her again.

Their father gave them
a big hug!

27

Puzzle time!

Which two words rhyme?

sad can ham jam hug

Which word does not match
the picture?

house

sweet

oven

Which word matches the picture?

page

cage

rage

Who pushes the witch?

Hansel

Gretel

aunty

Which sentence is right?

The bird ate the bread.

The cat ate the bread.

Puzzle time! Answers

Which two words rhyme? sad can ham (jam) hug

Which word does not match the picture? house sweet (oven)

Which word matches the picture? page (cage) rage

Who pushes the witch? Hansel (Gretel) aunty

Which sentence is right? (The bird ate the bread.) The cat ate the bread.